Uncle Max

Written by Roderick Hunt
Illustrated by Nick Schon,
based on the original characters
created by Roderick Hunt and Alex Brychta

D1391953

OXFORD
UNIVERSITY PRESS

Read these words

un**cle**	d**ow**n
c**oi**n	**ou**t
cl**ou**d	n**oi**se
t**oe**	g**o**

There was a noise outside the house.
An old car stopped with a bang and a big
cloud of smoke.

An odd-looking man got out. He had long, white hair, a flowing blue cloak and a big, green hat.

The man took out a huge case from the back of the car.

"Who is he?" asked Biff.

He's got odd shoes.

"He's my Uncle Max," said Dad. "I have not seen him since I was a little boy."

Is he a wizard?

"I have been in Peru, and all over the place," said Uncle Max, "but now I'm back."

"Nice to meet you," Uncle Max said to the children. "How do you do?"

10

"May I stay with you for a day or two?"
went on Uncle Max. "I won't be
a nuisance."

"Uncle Max has lots of cases," said Dad. "It may rain, so we need to get them inside."

Uncle Max had a parrot called Sue.
"She's quite shy," said Uncle Max.
"And she's quite rude," said Biff.

The children liked Uncle Max. He showed them a trick. He made a coin vanish.

"Look in your pockets," said Uncle Max. "See! Kipper has it."

Mum liked Uncle Max, too. He made a big pot of stew for dinner.

It looks yummy.

"It's made of dragons' tails and goblins' toes," said Uncle Max.

Uncle Max had a tale to tell.

"Sit down and I will tell you about my escape from a snake," he said.

"I was in Peru when a giant snake slid out of a tree. Its coils wound round me," said Uncle Max.

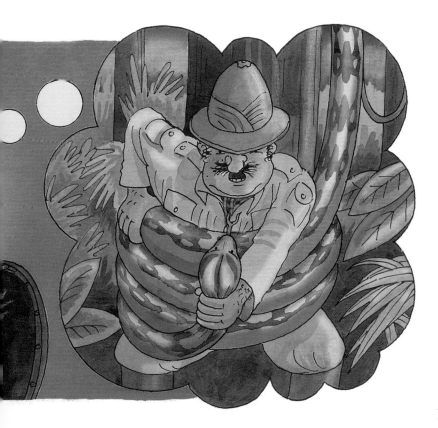

"But I knew the song of the snake,

… so I sang to it in a deep voice …

… the snake's coils unwound.

Then it lay on the ground and
went to sleep."

"This is my ice cream machine,"
said Uncle Max.

"What kind of ice cream would you like? I can make red, pink, blue or green."

The ice cream machine began to rattle and shake.

There was a flash and a bang.
The ice cream machine blew up.

"Look at my shed," said Dad.

"Er… do you fancy hot, black ice cream?" said Uncle Max.

"Time to go," said Uncle Max.
"I will come and stay again, soon."

Talk about the story

When did Dad last see Uncle Max?

What story did Uncle Max tell about the snake?

What did Mum and Dad think when the shed blew up?

What stories do you like to tell?

29

A maze

Help Uncle Max find his parrot.

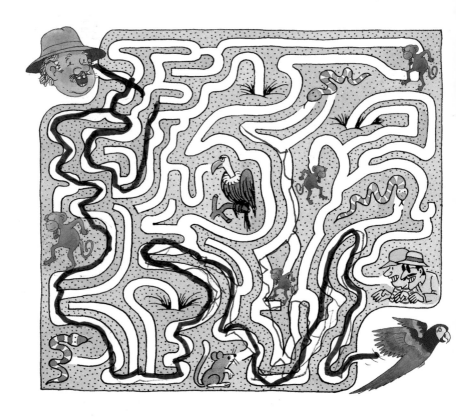